MUSEUM MIX-UP

by **Dorothy H. Price** illustrated by **Shiane Salabie**

PICTURE WINDOW BOOKS
a capstone imprint

Published by Picture Window Books, an imprint of Capstone.
1710 Roe Crest Drive, North Mankato, Minnesota 56003
capstonepub.com

Copyright © 2023 by Capstone.
All rights reserved. No part of this publication may be reproduced in whole or in part, or stored in a retrieval system, or transmitted in any form or by any means, electronic, mechanical, photocopying, recording, or otherwise, without written permission of the publisher.

Library of Congress Cataloging-in-Publication Data
Names: Price, Dorothy H., author. | Salabie, Shiane, illustrator.
Title: Museum mix-up / by Dorothy H. Price ; illustrated by Shiane Salabie.
Description: North Mankato, Minnesota : Picture Window Books, [2023] | Series: Jalen's big city life | Audience: Ages 5–7. | Audience: Grades K–1. | Summary: Seven-year-old J.C. is excited about the class field trip to the Famous Black Americans Museum, especially since his dad is coming along—and when his group gets separated from their teacher in the crowded museum, it is J.C. who remembers the map their teacher showed them and reunites the groups.
Identifiers: LCCN 2021047062 | ISBN 9781666334999 (hardcover) | ISBN 9781666335033 (paperback) | ISBN 9781666342000 (pdf) | ISBN 9781666342017 (kindle edition)
Subjects: LCSH: African American boys—Juvenile fiction. | School field trips—Juvenile fiction. | Fathers and sons—Juvenile fiction. | Museums—Juvenile fiction. | CYAC: School field trips—Fiction. | Museums—Fiction. | Fathers and sons—Fiction. | African Americans—Fiction. | LCGFT: Picture books.
Classification: LCC PZ7.1.P752828 Mu 2022 | DDC [E]—dc23
LC record available at https://lccn.loc.gov/2021047062

Editorial Credits
Editor: Alison Deering; Designer: Tracy Davies; Production Specialist: Katy LaVigne

Design Elements
Shutterstock: Alexzel, Betelejze, cuppuccino, wormig

TABLE OF CONTENTS

Chapter 1
CLASS TRIP 7

Chapter 2
FAMOUS FACES 12

Chapter 3
PAYING ATTENTION 19

Chapter 4
SOUVENIRS 23

MEET J.C.

Hi! My name is Jalen Corey Pierce, but everyone calls me J.C. I am seven years old. I live with Mom, Dad, and my baby sister, Maya. Nana and Pop-Pop live in our apartment building too. So do my two best friends, Amir and Vicky.

My family and I used to live in a small town. Now I live in a city with big buildings and lots of people. Come along with me on all my new adventures!

Chapter 1
CLASS TRIP

J.C. was excited to go to school. His class was going on a field trip! They were visiting the Famous Black Americans Museum.

"I can't wait for the class trip!" J.C. exclaimed.

J.C.'s dad was also going to the museum. He was an artist and excited to chaperone.

"Let's get going!" Dad said.

At school, J.C.'s teacher showed everyone a map of the museum.

"The museum might be crowded," Mrs. Rowe said. "Please stay together. I don't want anyone to get lost."

J.C. studied the map carefully. Then Mrs. Rowe split the class into groups.

"Group one will be with me," she said. "Group two will be with Mr. Pierce."

J.C. smiled at Amir and Vicky. They were all in the same group.

J.C.'s dad had been busy reading about a special new exhibit. It had wax figures of famous people.

"Oh!" he said. "Is it time? Is group two ready to rock and roll?"

"Yes!" they replied.

Chapter 2
FAMOUS FACES

Mrs. Rowe led the way to the subway. Everyone squeezed onto the train.

A few stops later, they reached the museum. The entrance was packed!

"I need to use the bathroom," Amir said.

"Mrs. Rowe, you can get started. We'll catch up," Dad said.

Group one started their tour. Amir went to the bathroom. Then Dad led the group toward the exhibit.

Each wax figure had a sign in front of it. The sign explained why the person was famous.

"That's Madam C.J. Walker," J.C. read.

"She was a very successful businesswoman," Dad explained.

"This one is Matthew Henson," Amir said.

"He was a great explorer," Dad told them. "And the first Black American to visit the North Pole."

"Over there!" Vicky pointed. "That's Kamala Harris."

"She is our first female vice president," Dad said. "She's also our first Black and Indian vice president."

"They all look so real!" Vicky added.

"They sure do," Dad agreed.

They reached the end of the first room. The hallway split in two directions. There were people *everywhere.*

"I don't see Mrs. Rowe or group one," Vicky said. She looked worried.

"Me neither," Amir added.

Dad looked worried too. "I'm all mixed up," he said. "Which way should we go?"

Chapter 3
PAYING ATTENTION

J.C. thought back to that morning at school. "I know!" he said. "We should go right."

"Are you sure?" Dad asked.

Vicky nodded. "Mrs. Rowe showed us the museum map in case we got lost."

"J.C. is right," said Amir. "Right is right."

"I guess I should have listened more carefully," Dad said. "I'm glad you all paid attention!"

Group two kept right and continued the tour. They saw figures of Cicely Tyson, Maya Angelou, and Barack Obama.

They passed lots of other classes and groups. But they didn't see group one. Finally . . .

"There they are!" J.C. pointed.

Dad and group two walked fast to catch up.

"You finally found us," said Mrs. Rowe.

"Thanks to my group," Dad said. "They remembered the museum map you showed us."

"It's good to know everyone paid attention," Mrs. Rowe replied.

Chapter 4
SOUVENIRS

The groups stayed close together for the rest of the tour. There were no more mix-ups.

When it was over, everyone stopped in the museum gift shop.

"Does anyone want to buy a souvenir?" Mrs. Rowe asked.

"I like this Madam C.J. Walker key chain. I want to be successful like her," J.C. said.

"This Matthew Henson snow globe is cool. I want to visit the North Pole one day," Amir said.

"I'll buy this Kamala Harris pin," Vicky said. "I want to be vice president when I grow up. And then president!"

"Those are wonderful ideas," Dad replied.

"Let's thank Mr. Pierce for chaperoning our class trip," said Mrs. Rowe.

"Thank you, Mr. Pierce!" the class said.

Dad laughed. "You're all welcome. Now, who knows how to get home?"

GLOSSARY

chaperone (SHAP-uh-rohn)—a person who goes with and is responsible for a group of young people

exhibit (ig-ZIH-buht)—a display that usually includes objects and information to teach people about a certain subject

famous (FEY-muhs)—very well-known

figure (FIG-yer)—a sculpted shape made to look like a real person

millionaire (mil-yuh-NAIR)—a rich person who has at least one million dollars

museum (myoo-ZEE-uhm)—a place where objects of art, history, or science are shown

souvenir (soo-vuh-NIHR)—an object that is kept as a reminder of a special event

wax (waks)—a yellowish, sticky substance that is soft and easily shaped when warm

FAMOUS FIGURES

Select one of the famous Black Americans mentioned in the story. Do some research to learn something new about that person. You can find information online or at the library. Then, draw a picture of the person you chose doing something you learned about.

1. Have you ever visited a museum? Where was it, and what did you see? What did you like most about the visit? Was there anything you didn't like?

2. Mrs. Rowe showed J.C. and the other kids a map of the museum in case someone got lost. Have you ever been lost or separated on a class trip? Did you know what to do?

3. There were many famous Black Americans in the wax exhibit at the museum. With your friends or family, talk about some other famous Black Americans J.C.'s class might have seen during the tour.

1. J.C.'s class was split into two groups. Would you have wanted to be in group one with Mrs. Rowe or group two with J.C.'s dad? Explain why.

2. J.C., Amir, and Vicky each buy a different souvenir. Which person mentioned in the story would you have wanted a souvenir of? Why?

3. The famous Black Americans at the museum inspired J.C. and his friends to think about what they want to do one day. Think about the accomplishments mentioned in the story. Then make a list of things you would like to do when you grow up.

ABOUT THE CREATORS

Dorothy H. Price loves writing stories for young readers, starting with her first picture book, *Nana's Favorite Things*. A 2019 winner of the We Need Diverse Books Mentorship Program, Dorothy is also an active member of the SCBWI Carolinas. She hopes all young readers know they can grow up to write stories too.

Shiane Salabie is a Jamaica-born illustrator based in the Philadelphia tri-state area. When she moved to the United States, she discovered her first true love: the library. Shiane later realized that she wanted to bring stories to life and uses her art to do so.